MW01610386

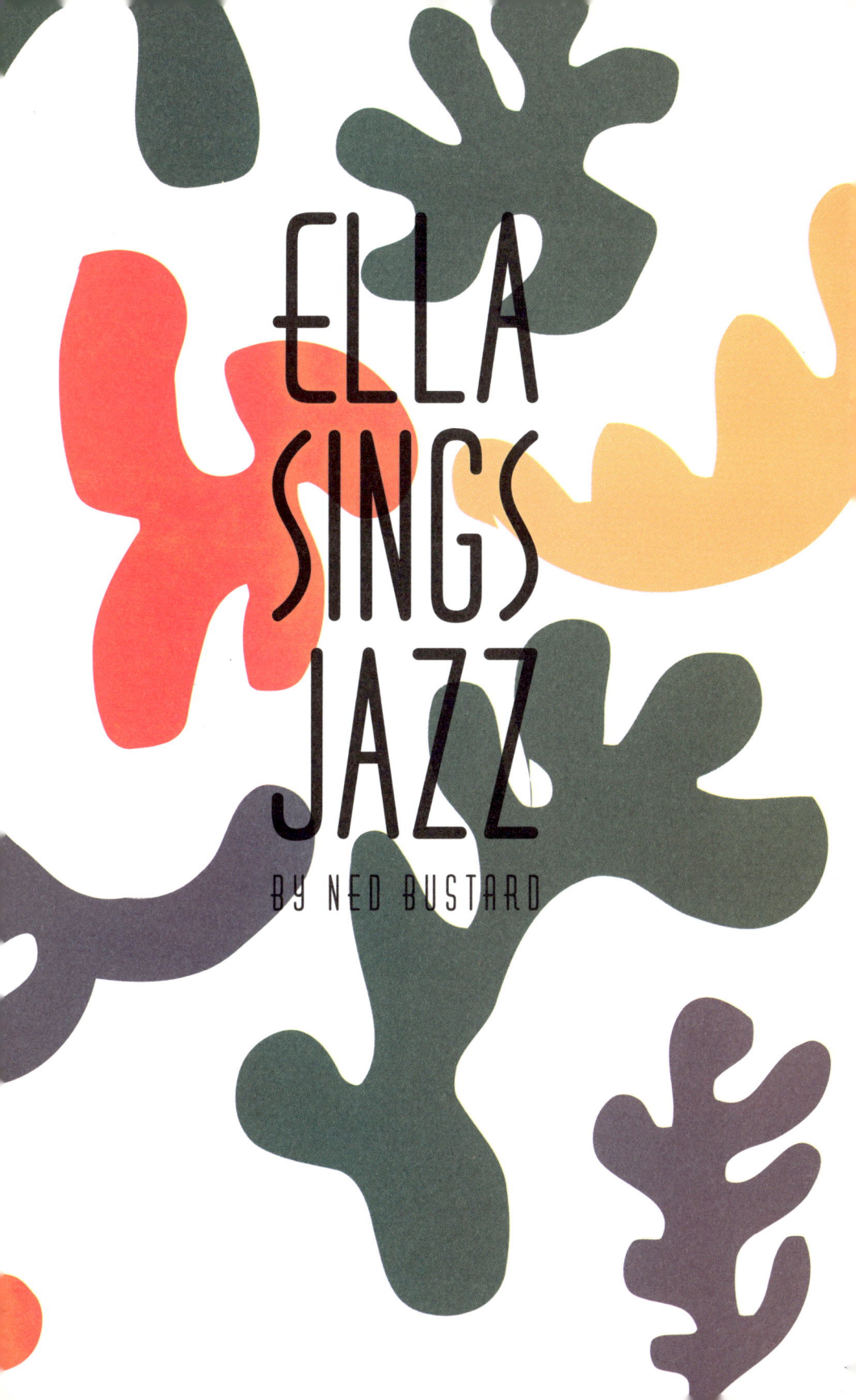

ELLA SINGS JAZZ

BY NED BUSTARD

Veritas Press
1250 Belle Meade Drive
Lancaster, PA 17601

First edition

ELLA SINGS JAZZ

BY NED BUSTARD

THIS BOOK
IS DEDICATED
TO LESLIE
—BECAUSE
IT IS HER
FAVORITE.

Ella had fun singing.

When Ella was set to sing,
she sang with Chick Webb.
Chick was the king of
"swing."

He and Ella got the hall hopping.
All the gang were huffing and
puffing, dipping and rocking to the
swinging songs. There was no
napping when Ella was singing.

It was not long and Ella was getting to sing "jazz" songs. Ella sang jazz songs in big and not-so-big halls.

Then Ella sang "pop" songs.
Ella's pop singing set the fans to
buzzing. Then the fans were
begging for Ella's pop singing!

Ella was itching to go back to jazz singing. Ella got a job singing the budding jazz of "bebop."

Bebop was not like pop or swing.
Ella sang bebop songs by singing,
"Bah bah bah nop do bo de do."

Bebop songs were not catching on. Fans did not like bebop singing, but Ella sang, "Bing bang bong, ping pang pong, and do bo bo bah bah bah nop do bo de do."

Ella's bebop singing set the fans to humming. Ella was winning fans with the zinging singing. Then the fans were begging for Ella's bebop singing!

Ella was running to this hall and that, for fans were loving the singing. They said that Ella had the top lungs for singing.

Ella sang bebop, jazz, pop and swing like no one sang. When Ella had sung a song, the song was sung the tip top.

Ella had fun singing.